WHAT HAPPENS WHEN
I go to the
DOCTOR

Written by Helen Slater
Illustrated by Lyn Mitchell

Mary does not feel well today. She has a sore throat and her head hurts.

Mommy feels Mary's forehead. "You feel hot," she says. "I'm taking Jake to the doctor this morning. You can come too." Daddy phones the school to say Mary is sick.

At the doctor's, Mommy tells the secretary that they have come to see Doctor Brown.

"We must sit in the waiting room until the doctor is ready to see us," Mommy tells Mary.

The secretary looks for Mary and Jake's notes.
Every time that Mary and Jake visit the doctor,
the doctor writes down what is wrong.

After a while, the secretary tells Mary's mother
that Doctor Brown is ready to see them. They go
into the doctor's room.

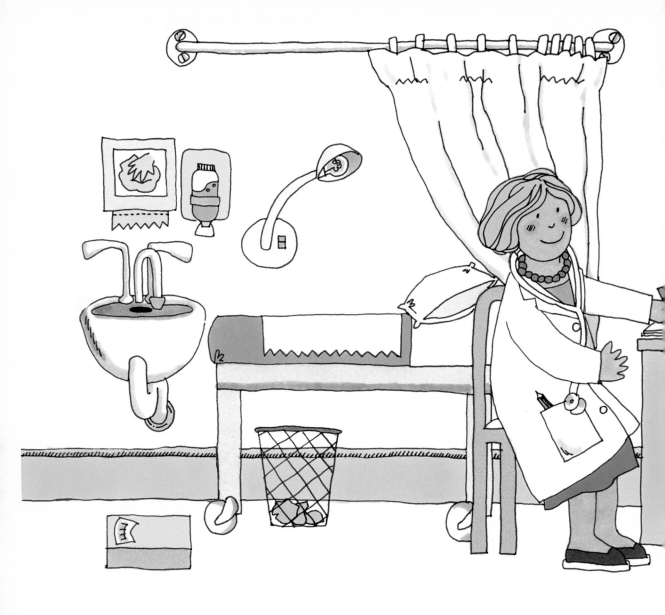

This is the doctor's examining room. Doctor Brown
says to Mary, "Now tell me how you feel today."

Mary tells the doctor about her sore throat and headache. Doctor Brown writes down everything on Mary's special notes.

Doctor Brown gently feels
Mary's neck to see if
it hurts at all. Mary says
it doesn't.

Then the doctor looks
at Mary's throat.
"Open wide and say
AAAAH," says the doctor.

Next, the doctor uses a stethoscope to listen to Mary's chest. ''Take a big breath, Mary,'' she says.

Now Doctor Brown uses a special light like a tiny flashlight to look inside Mary's ears.

Doctor Brown writes on a piece of paper. "This is a prescription," she tells Mary. "Mommy will take it to the drugstore, and get some medicine for you."

Jake cut his elbow last week and now it's time to take off the bandage. "It has healed very well," says the doctor.

Time to go. Mary and Jake say goodbye to the secretary as they go out the door.

On the way home, they go into the drugstore.
Mommy gives the prescription to the pharmacist.

The pharmacist fills a bottle with orange syrup, and puts a label on the front.

The pharmacist shows the label to Mommy. "Give Mary one spoonful of syrup three times a day," he says.

When they get home again, Daddy gives Mary
a spoonful of her medicine before she goes to bed.

Mary feels a little better the next day. Jake says that Teddy is not well, so Mary gives him a pretend spoonful of medicine.

Soon Mary is well again and can go back to school. "Do you know," she tells Mommy, "when I grow up, I'm going to be a doctor!"